D0860201

A DINO EASY READER

Rex and Lilly
Playtime

Stories by Laurie Krasny Brown
Pictures by Marc Brown

Little, Brown and Company
Boston   New York   Toronto   London

For all the champion teachers and readers
at Derby Academy

Copyright © 1995 by Laurene Krasny Brown and Marc Brown

All rights reserved. No part of this book may be reproduced in any form or by any electronic or mechanical means, including information storage and retrieval systems, without permission in writing from the publisher, except by a reviewer who may quote brief passages in a review.

First Edition
A Dino Easy Reader and the Dinosaur logo are trademarks of Little,
Brown and Company.
Library of Congress Cataloging-in-Publication Data
Brown, Laurene Krasny.
    Rex and Lilly playtime / stories by Laurie Krasny Brown ;
pictures by Marc Brown. — 1st ed.
        p.   cm. — (A Dino easy reader)
    Summary: Dinosaur siblings Rex and Lilly play at various activities.
    ISBN 0-316-11386-7
    1. Brothers and sisters — Fiction. [1. Dinosaurs — Fiction.
    2. Play — Fiction.] I. Brown, Marc Tolon, ill. II. Title.
    III. Series: Brown, Laurene Krasny. Dino easy reader.
    PZ7.B816114Rd   1995
    [E] — dc20   93-25877

                    10 9 8 7 6 5 4 3 2 1
                                WOR
                    Published simultaneously in Canada
                    by Little, Brown & Company (Canada) Limited

                    Printed in the United States of America

Contents

Copycat

"Now, don't copy me, Rex!" said Lilly.

"Up I go! Down I go!

In I go! Whee!"

"But I want to slide in, too!" said Rex.

"Up I go! Down I go!

In I go! Whee!"

"Don't copy me this time, Rex!" said Lilly.

"Step back, Rex. Ready?

In I go! Whee!"

"But I want to jump in, too!" said Rex.

"Step back, Lilly," said Rex. "Ready?

In I go!"

"Bet you can't go in like this!" said Rex.

"Yes, I can!" said Lilly. "I'll show you."

"I can go in like this, too!" said Lilly.

"See?"

Let's Dance

"Time for dance class, Rex," said Mom.

"Let's go now."

"Not me! Not now!" said Rex.

"I don't want to dance."

"Just try!" said Mom.

"How shall we warm up?" the dance

teacher, Ms. Tiptoe, asked the class.

"Push-ups," said Rose.

"Jumping jacks," said Jack.

"Hot cocoa," said Rex.

The class warmed up.

They did push-ups.

They did jumping jacks.

Rex warmed up, too.

"Time to dance now!" said Ms. Tiptoe.

"I will show you how.

Boys, you dance *forward step, back step,*

slide, slide, slide.

Girls, you dance *back step, forward step,*

slide, slide, slide."

"Now you try! Ready?" said Ms. Tiptoe.

The boys did the steps.

The girls did the steps.

Rex did the steps, too.

"Good!" said Ms. Tiptoe. "Girls,

please pick a boy to dance with."

"Not me! Not now!" said Rex.

Then Rose asked Rex, "Will you dance with me?"

ICE

"Me? Now?" asked Rex.

"Yes!" said Rose.

"Now for the music," said Ms. Tiptoe.

"Let's dance!"

Rose danced *back step, forward step,*

slide, slide, slide.

Rex danced *forward step, back step,*

slide, slide, slide.

They danced on and on.

"See you next time, boys and girls!"

 said Ms. Tiptoe.

"Let's go, Rex," said Mom.

"Not me! Not now!" said Rex.

"I did try, and I do want to dance!"

Dress-Up

"Mom, may we go out?" asked Lilly.

"We want to play ball!" said Rex.

"No, a ball game is not play

for a rainy day," said Mom.

"What can we do?" asked Rex.

"We can play dress-up!" said Lilly.

"Dress-up is play for a rainy day."

"I know!" said Rex. "I can dress up

to play ball!"

"What can I put on?" said Lilly.

"Ready yet?" asked Rex.

"Ready!" said Lilly.

"Let's go show Mom."

"How do we look?" asked Lilly.

"You look ready to play ball," said Mom.

"Now may we go out?" asked Rex.

"No," said Mom. "A ball game is not play

for a rainy day."

"Rats!" said Rex.

"I still want to play ball."

"I know what we can do," said Lilly.

"What now?" said Rex.

Step out.

"Ready yet?" asked Lilly.

"Ready!" said Rex.

"How do we look now?" asked Lilly.

"You look ready to play ball in the rain!"

said Mom.

"Now may we go out?" asked Rex.

"Yes!" said Mom. "A ball game

can be play for a rainy day!"

NORTHEAST
SPRUILL OAKS

J EASY BROWN   **NE FUL**
Brown, Laurie Krasny
Rex and Lilly playtime

Atlanta-Fulton Public Library